PINKY and REX
Get Married

OTHER BOOKS
BY JAMES HOWE

PICTURE BOOKS
There's a Monster Under My Bed
There's a Dragon in My Sleeping Bag

PINKY AND REX BOOKS
Pinky and Rex
Pinky and Rex Go to Camp
Pinky and Rex and the Spelling Bee
Pinky and Rex and the Mean Old Witch
Pinky and Rex and the New Baby
Pinky and Rex and the Double Dad Weekend
Pinky and Rex and the Bully
Pinky and Rex and the New Neighbors
Pinky and Rex and the School Play
Pinky and Rex and the Perfect Pumpkin

BUNNICULA BOOKS
Bunnicula
Howliday Inn
The Celery Stalks at Midnight
Nighty-Nightmare
Return to Howliday Inn

SEBASTIAN BARTH MYSTERIES
What Eric Knew
Stage Fright
Eat Your Poison, Dear
Dew Drop Dead

MIDDLE GRADE FICTION
Morgan's Zoo
A Night Without Stars
The Teddy Bear's Scrapbook

PINKY and REX
Get Married
by James Howe
illustrated by Melissa Sweet

Ready-to-Read

Simon Spotlight

First Aladdin Paperbacks edition May 1999
First Simon Spotlight paperback edition September 2012

Simon Spotlight
An imprint of Simon & Schuster
Children's Publishing Division
1230 Avenue of the Americas
New York, NY 10020

The Library of Congress has cataloged the hardcover edition as follows:
Howe, James, 1946-
Pinky and Rex get married / by James Howe; illustrated by Melissa Sweet. —1st ed.
p.   cm.
Summary: Rex and her best friend Pinky decide that
they like each other enough to get married,
and all their stuffed toys and dinosaurs
appear as guests at the wedding.
ISBN 978-0-689-31453-7 (hc.)
[1. Weddings—Fiction. 2. Friendship—Fiction.]
I. Sweet, Melissa, ill. II. Title.
PZ7.H83727Pj   1990
[E]—dc19   89-406
ISBN 978-0-689-82526-2 (pbk.)
1118 LAK

To my niece, Jennifer
—J. H.

For Billy
—M. S.

Contents

Chapter 1

Where Is Rex?

"Where are you going?" Pinky's mother asked.

"Outside," called Pinky. "I'm going to play with Rex."

It was a beautiful day, a perfect day for playing outside. What would they do? he wondered, as he waited to cross the street. Maybe they would

ride their bikes. Maybe they
would climb the new jungle gym in
Rex's backyard. Or maybe they would
tell each other knock-knock jokes
and laugh even at the ones they had
heard before. Whatever they did,
Pinky knew it would be fun because
they would be doing it together.

When he got to Rex's house, he was surprised to find that the front door was closed. The back door was closed, too. And all the windows were shut tight.

"No one is home," he said sadly. He sat down on the steps and rested his head in his hands.

"Where's Rex?" he heard someone say. Looking up, Pinky saw his little sister, Amanda, standing at the curb on the other side of the street.

"I don't know," he said. "I want to play with her, but she isn't here."

"Play with me then," said Amanda.

Pinky didn't want to play with his sister. But he also didn't know when Rex would come home, and it was too nice a day to waste.

"All right," he said. "What do you want to do?"

"Let's play on Rex's jungle gym," Amanda said.

Pinky knew that Rex wouldn't mind if he and Amanda played on her new jungle gym. So he walked across the street, took his sister by

4

the hand, crossed the street again,
and ran with her into Rex's backyard.

Amanda loved the jungle gym. She laughed even when she fell onto the grass. But Pinky didn't laugh, even when he flipped upside down and felt his insides tickle. He didn't laugh, because he was *not* having a good time.

I'd have more fun with Rex, he thought. Where *is* she?

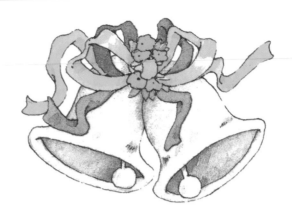

Chapter 2
Pinky's Idea

Soon it was time to go home for lunch. After they ate, Amanda told Pinky she wanted to go back to Rex's house to play on the jungle gym.

"I don't think so," said Pinky. "I think I'll ride my bike."

"Not fair," Amanda whined. "You go too fast for me, Pinky."

Pinky smiled.

All afternoon, he rode his bike. But no matter how far he rode or how fast he went, Pinky still wasn't having fun. Things just weren't the same without Rex.

He was about to go home when
he spotted a car pulling into the
driveway across the street. Rex got

out of the car. She was all dressed up.
"Where *were* you?" Pinky shouted.
He dropped his bike and ran to her.

"At a wedding," said Rex. "Don't you remember? I told you I was going to a wedding today."

"You did?"

"Oh, Pinky," Rex said, shaking her head, "you forget everything!"

This made Pinky feel even worse. Not only was he sad from missing Rex, now he felt silly that he had forgotten where she was. Rex saw the look on his face. "Don't feel bad, Pinky," she said. "It doesn't matter if you forget things. I like you just the same." Then she held out some flowers. "Look what I got. The bride threw these, and I caught them. Do you know what that means?"

Pinky shrugged his shoulders.

"I'll get married soon," Rex said, laughing. "Isn't that funny, Pinky?"

12

"Yes," he said, but he didn't laugh. "Can we play now?" he asked.

"Okay," said Rex. "What do you want to do? We can play on my jungle gym."

Pinky shook his head.

"I could get my bike."

Pinky shook his head some more. He had been riding for a long time and he was tired.

"What will we do then?" Rex asked.

"*I* have an idea," said Pinky.

"What?"

"Let's get married."

Chapter 3
Getting Ready

It was not easy for Pinky to keep his idea a secret from Amanda.

"Where are you taking *those*?" she wanted to know, when she saw Pinky carrying all his stuffed animals across the street to Rex's house.

"Nowhere," said Pinky.

"Why are you wearing *that*?" she asked, when she saw Pinky putting on his best pink tie.

"No reason," Pinky answered.

"Why can't *I* play?" she wailed,
when Pinky crossed the street and
left her standing at the curb.
"Because," he told her.

Pinky and Rex decided to get
married in the garden behind Rex's
house. Rex explained that the friends
of the man sit on one side, and the
friends of the woman sit on the

18

other. So Pinky lined up all his
animals along one side of the path
that led to the garden. And Rex
placed all her dinosaurs on the other.
"Who will marry us?" Rex asked.

Pinky looked at all his animals. "Pretzel," he said, picking out his favorite. Rex wasn't sure she wanted to be married by a pig, but then she thought of how much Pinky loved him. And that made it all right.

"We have to have rings," she said then.

"I don't have any money," said Pinky. "Besides, all the ring stores will be closed."

"We can make them," Rex suggested. She bent down and pulled out some long, thick blades of grass. "Twist them around each other, and they'll be our rings."

"What about music?" asked Pinky.

Rex ran inside the house and came out with her tape player. "I picked out my favorite song," she said. "We can play it while I march down the aisle. Oh-oh."

"What's wrong?"

"I have to wear a veil."

"No, you don't," said Pinky. "You look nice in your party dress."

"But I *have* to have a veil," Rex insisted. She ran into the house again and came out with a sheet.

"Mother says there are no curtains I can play with, but she gave me this sheet. It will just have to do."

Pinky helped Rex put the sheet
over her head. She couldn't see
through it, so he agreed to help her
walk down the aisle. He started the
music and put the flowers in Rex's
hand.

"Is everything pretty?" Rex asked.
"Yes," said Pinky. "And all the
guests are smiling."

Chapter 4
The Wedding

Pinky and Rex walked down the
path to the rosebushes. Pinky made
sure Rex didn't trip on the sheet.
When they got to where Pretzel was
propped up against a large rock, they
stopped.

"What do we do now?" Pinky asked.

"We say things," said Rex.

"Say things? Like what?"

"Like why we're getting married and stuff."

"Oh." Pinky thought, but he didn't know what he should say. At last he said, "You first."

"Let's see," Rex said, from under the sheet. "Okay. I'm marrying you, Pinky, because you are my best friend. And I missed you today."

"You did?" Pinky asked.

The sheet nodded up and down.

"I missed you, too," Pinky told Rex. "And I'm marrying you because…because…oh, I know. Knock, knock."

"Who's there?"
"Olive."

"Olive who?"
"Olive you."

Pinky could not see Rex's face, but
he heard her giggle, so he knew she
liked what he had said. He took her
hand and put the grass ring on her
finger. And then, because Rex
couldn't see to do it, he put his ring
on his own finger. "Now what?"
he asked.

"Pretzel has to say we're married."

Pinky picked Pretzel up and said
in his best pig voice, "I say that you,
Pinky, and you, Rex, are now
married."

"Now we kiss," Rex said.

Pinky dropped Pretzel into the
bushes. *"What?"* he cried.

Rex pulled back the cloth from her

face. "It's hot under here," she said. She saw Pinky's cheeks turning red. "Well, we *have* to kiss," she told him. "Or we aren't married."

"Well, if we have to," he said. He kissed Rex lightly on the cheek, and she kissed him on the nose.

After that, they had a party with all
the animals and all the dinosaurs, and
then it was time for Pinky to go home.

Chapter 5
Married Life

"What are you wearing on your finger?" Pinky's father asked him at dinner that night.

"A ring," said Pinky.

"What did you do today?" his mother asked.

"Rex and I got married," he said.

"*I* want to get married, too!" Amanda wailed.

"Well," said Pinky's mother, passing the potatoes, "I'm afraid you just aren't old enough, Amanda. You will have to wait until you are at least seven."

Amanda put down her fork and crossed her arms. "Not fair," she mumbled.

"And are you going to have any children?" Pinky's father asked.

"Twins," said Pinky. "A boy and a girl. I'm going to stay home and take care of them, while Rex goes out to work. We had a long talk."

Pinky's parents smiled at him.

"Amanda," Pinky's mother said,

"please stop pouting and eat your carrots."

No one had to remind Pinky to eat *his* carrots. He was married now and very grown-up. He ate everything on his plate.

Just before bedtime, Pinky went out to the front porch of his house and called Rex's name. When she appeared at her window, he pointed to the ring on his finger. She pointed to the ring on her finger. Then they waved good-night. And Pinky came inside and went upstairs to bed.